# Usborne
# BIG STICKER BOOK
# BUGS

Illustrated by **Rebecca Mills**

Written by **Alice James**

Designed by
**Josephine Thompson**
and **Ian McNee**

With expert advice from
**Zoë M. Simmons**

## Contents

2  Enter the bug world
4  Sneaky spiders
6  Bugs in the night
8  Whooshing wings
10 Weird and wonderful
12 Big bugs

14 Buzzing bees
16 Growing and changing
18 Scuttle, scuttle
20 Tarantula!
22 Clever camouflage
24 Spot the bug

At the back of this book, you will find lots of stickers.

The bugs in this book are not drawn exactly to scale.

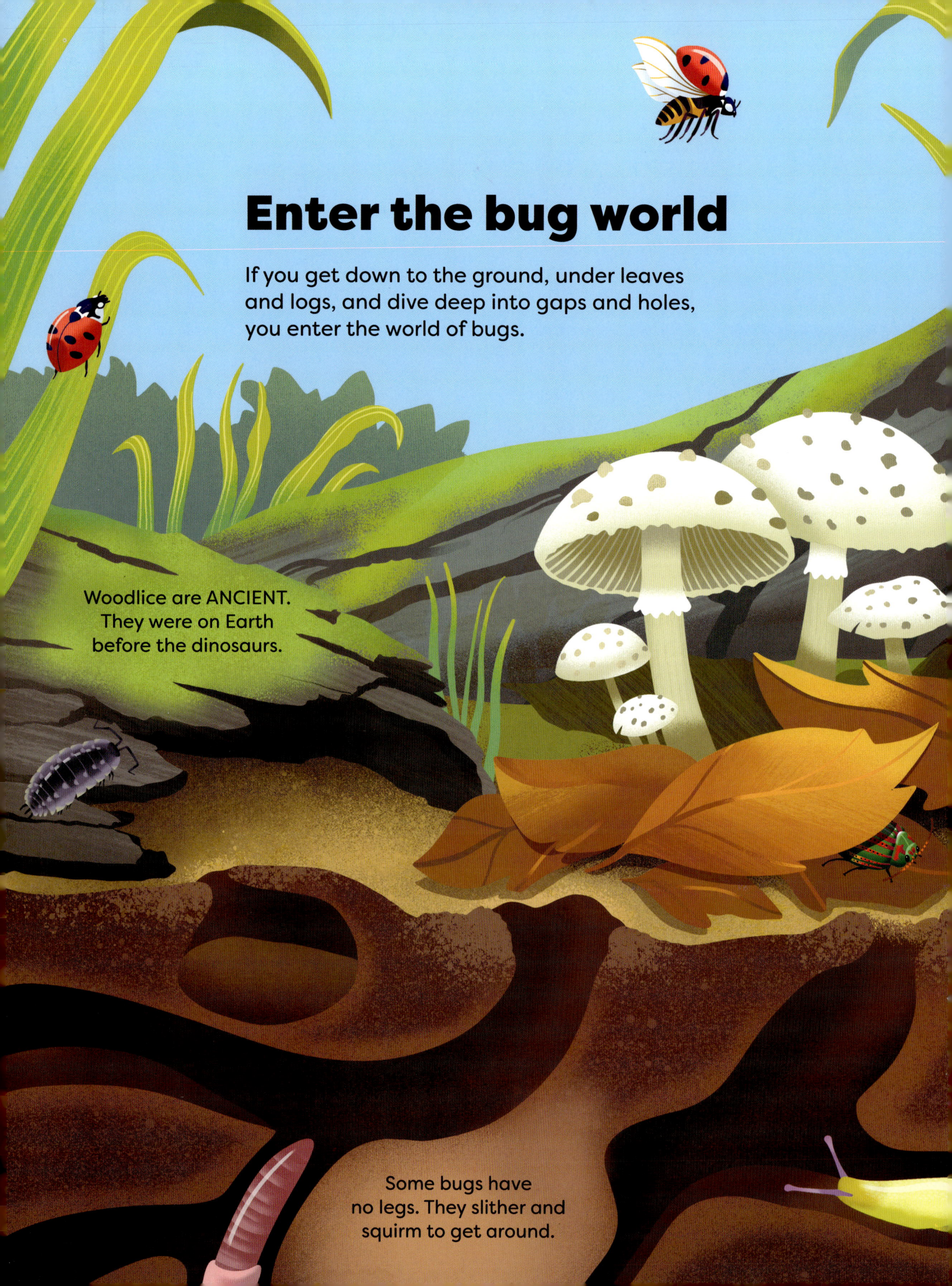

# Enter the bug world

If you get down to the ground, under leaves and logs, and dive deep into gaps and holes, you enter the world of bugs.

Woodlice are ANCIENT. They were on Earth before the dinosaurs.

Some bugs have no legs. They slither and squirm to get around.

# Sneaky spiders

Spiders are a type of bug called ARACHNIDS, which have eight legs. Many spiders build webs out of sticky strands and catch their food in them. Fill these webs with spiders.

Spider webs are made from silk, spun from inside the spider's body.

Animals that come out at night are called NOCTURNAL animals.

# Whooshing wings

The air above this pond is filled with the whirring of mayflies, dragonflies and damselflies. But they start life in the water.

Many baby insects are called NYMPHS. Dragonfly, damselfly and mayfly nymphs all live in the water. They only fly as adults.

The adults live for a matter of days. That's just long enough to lay thousands of eggs, which will turn into more nymphs.

# Weird and wonderful

Bugs come in an extraordinary variety of shapes and sizes, from teeny-tiny to big and hairy. Nowhere is the range bigger than in the depths of the hot jungle.

Leafhopper nymphs like this one have huge, shimmering tails.

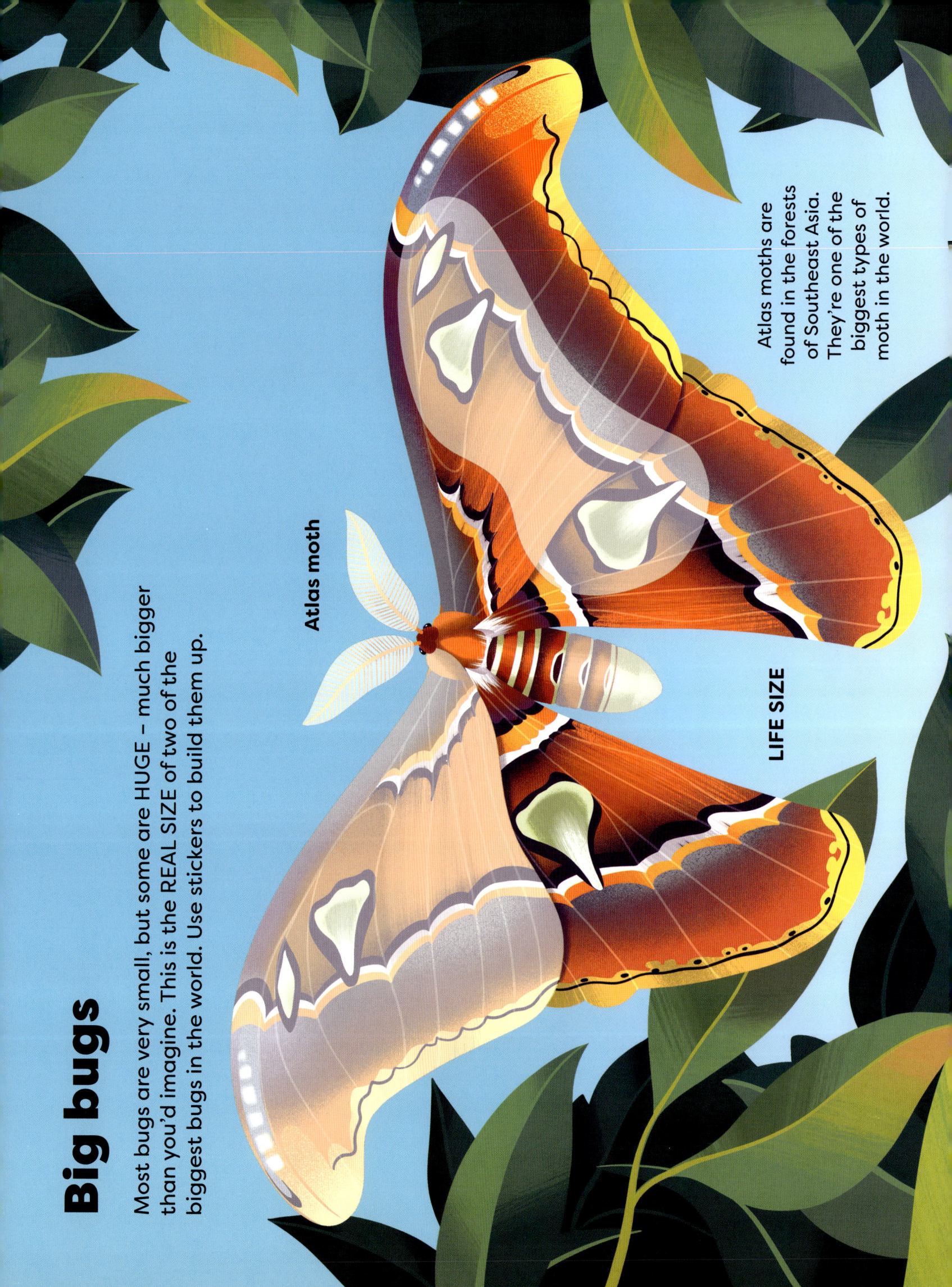

# Big bugs

Most bugs are very small, but some are HUGE – much bigger than you'd imagine. This is the REAL SIZE of two of the biggest bugs in the world. Use stickers to build them up.

**Atlas moth**

**LIFE SIZE**

Atlas moths are found in the forests of Southeast Asia. They're one of the biggest types of moth in the world.

Wētā are a group of giant insects, all found in New Zealand. They are the heaviest insects in the world.

LIFE SIZE

Wētā

# Growing and changing

Many bugs change through their lives, like caterpillars, which grow up to be butterflies. Add caterpillars to the leaves and fill the air with flying butterflies.

When bugs change completely, it's called METAMORPHOSIS. The babies are called LARVAE.

Butterflies are some of the brightest and most beautiful bugs. They fly with their wings open, and perch with their wings closed.

# Scuttle, scuttle

These scuttling bugs in the undergrowth are called MYRIAPODS, which means lots of legs. Add some in here.

All these bugs have bodies divided up into chunks called segments.

# Tarantula!

This is a tarantula – a huge, hairy spider. Add in the missing parts of its body.

Use the stickers to build up and complete this tarantula.

This is a Mexican red knee tarantula. This picture is bigger than life size – but not by much!

This tarantula's sting comes from its furry hairs. It can flick them off its legs and make an attacker itch and sting.

**Giant katydid**

**Crab spider**

**Peppered moth**

# Spot the bug

Bugs come in an INCREDIBLE range of shapes.
Add a sticker for each of these.
Can you spot them in the book?

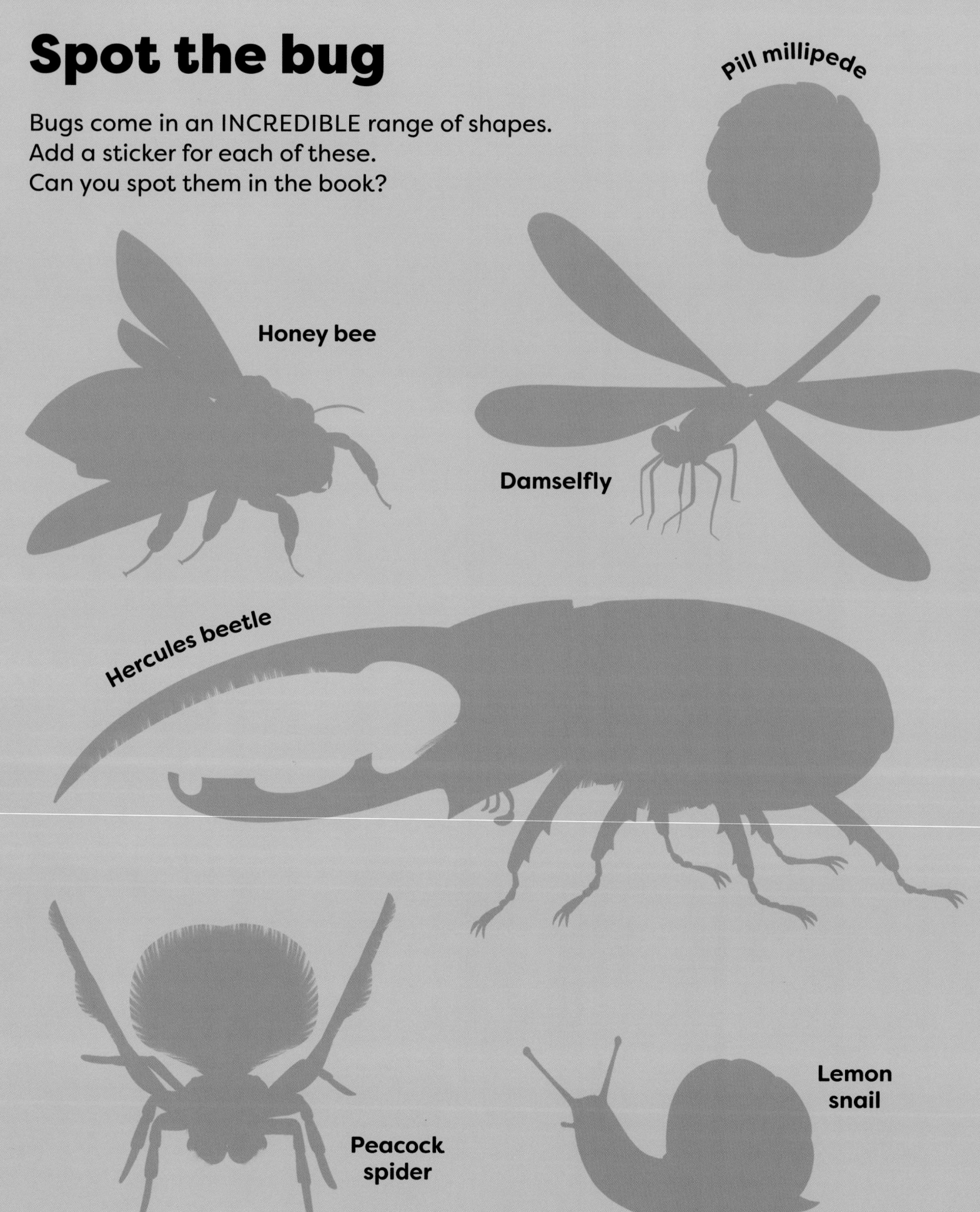

Pill millipede

Honey bee

Damselfly

Hercules beetle

Peacock spider

Lemon snail

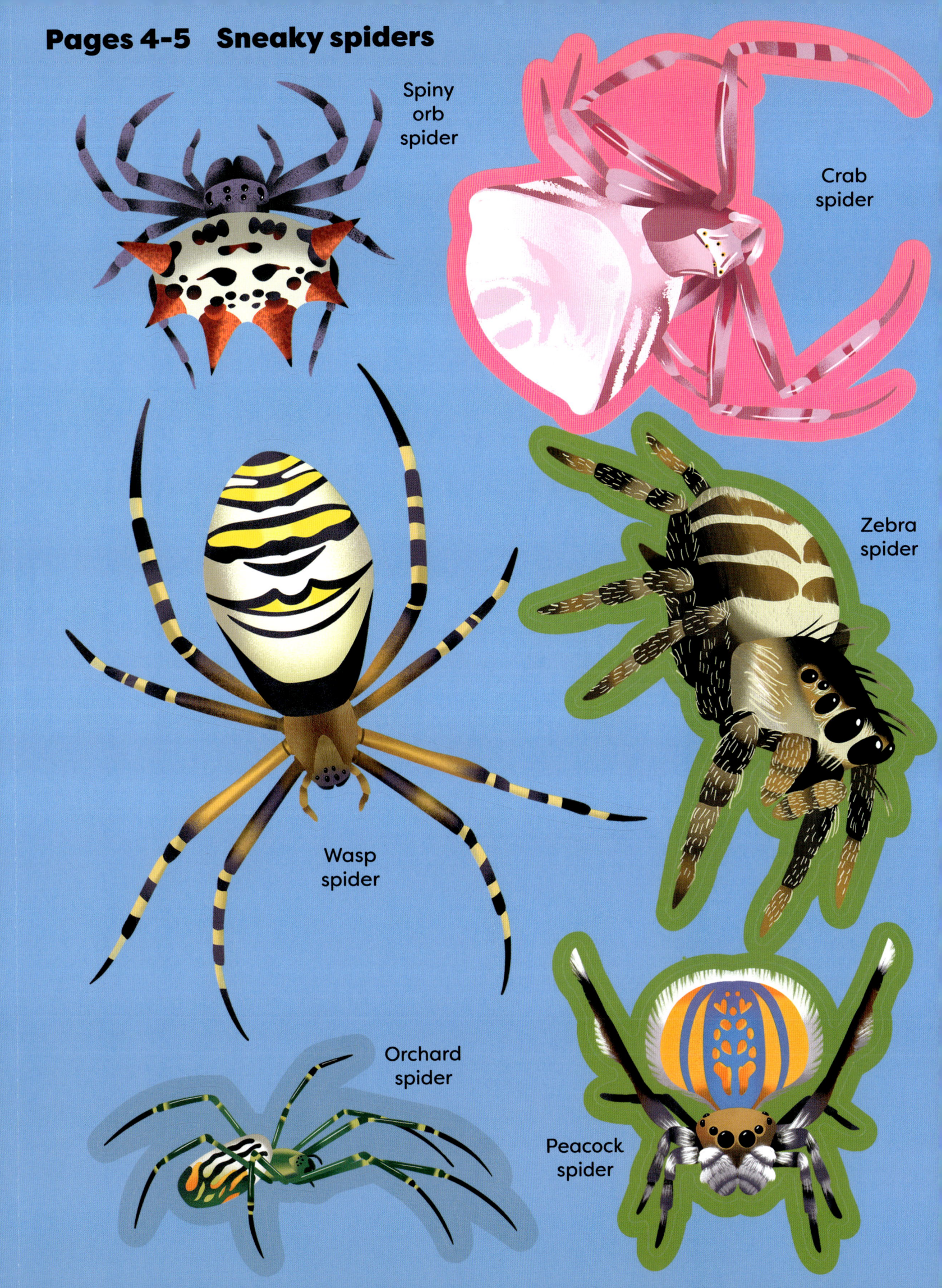

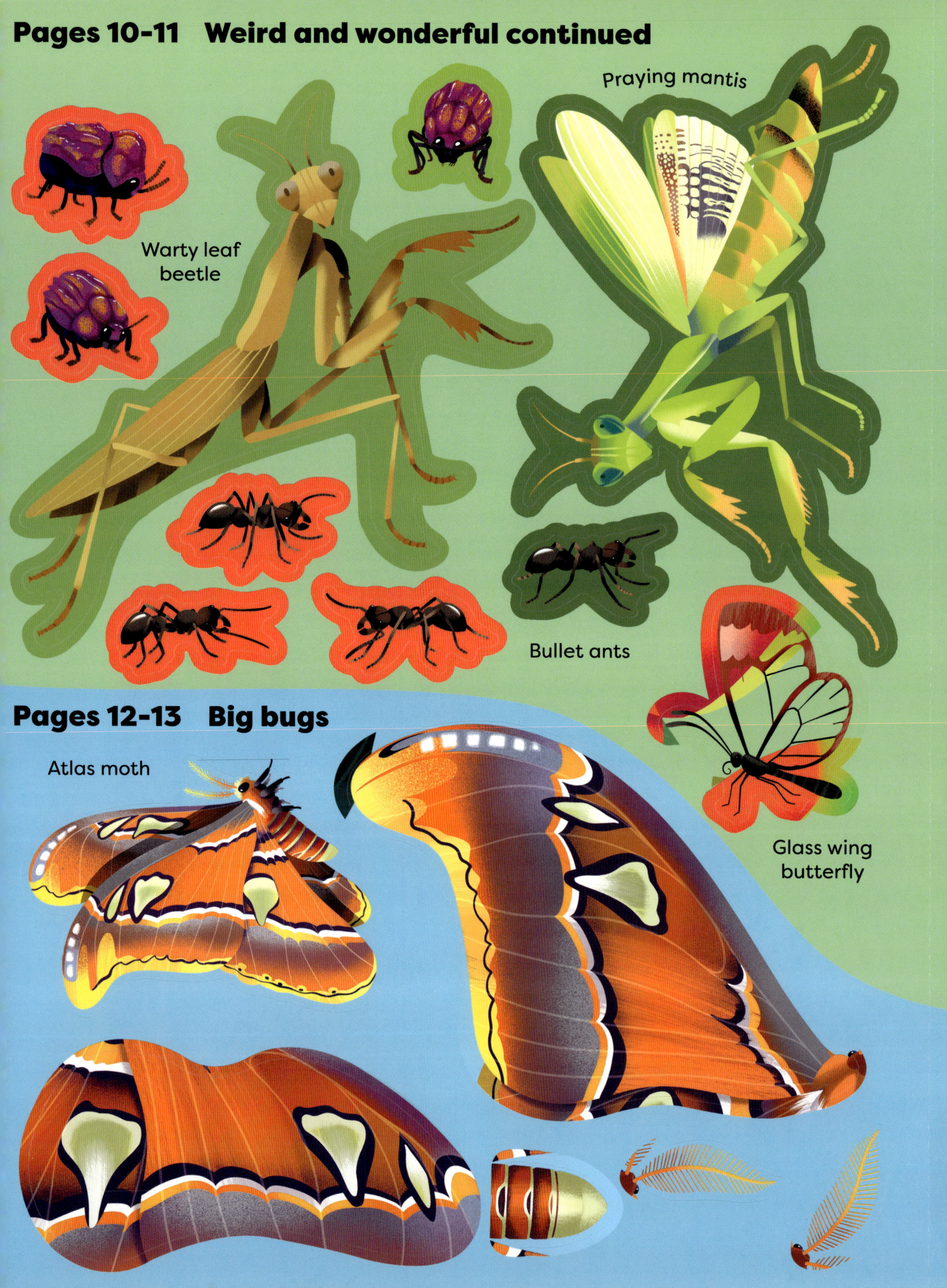

# Pages 16-17  Growing and changing